Story based on the characters from Max Lucado's *Hermie: A Common Caterpillar.*
Visit us at: www.hermieandfriends.com
Email us at: comments@hermieandfriends.com

Illustrations by GlueWorks Animation.

Published in Nashville, Tennessee, by Tommy Nelson®, a Division of Thomas
Nelson, Inc.

The publisher thanks June Ford, Amy Parker, Troy Schmidt, Holly Gusick, and
Kathleen Vaghy for their assistance in the preparation of this book.

Library of Congress Cataloging-in-Publication Data

Lucado, Max.
  Numbers / illustrations by GlueWorks Animation.
      p. cm. — (Buginnings)
  Based on the characters from Max Lucado's Hermie, a common caterpillar.
  Summary: When Hermie sets out to collect some of God's beautiful things in a
basket, he needs some help from his friends.
  ISBN 1-4003-0418-0 (hardback)
  [1. Caterpillars—Fiction. 2. Christian life—Fiction. 3. Counting.] I. GlueWorks
Animation. II. Series.
  PZ7.L9684Num 2004
  [E]—dc22   2003028180

Printed in The United States of America
04 05 06 07 08 PHX 5 4 3 2 1

Buginnings

NUMBERS

Based on the characters from Max Lucado's
Hermie: A Common Caterpillar

Tommy NELSON®

www.tommynelson.com

A Division of Thomas Nelson, Inc.
www.ThomasNelson.com

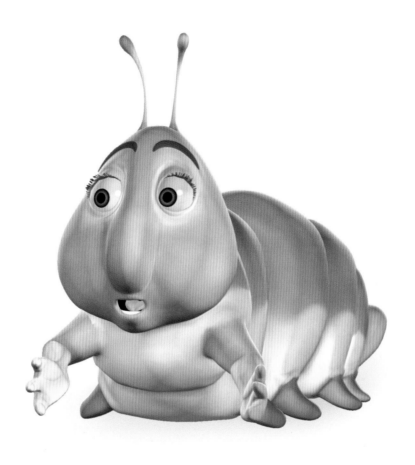

"Hermie, what is that on your back?" Wormie asked.

"A basket," said Hermie. "God made so many great things. I'm going to see how many I can collect in my basket. Come with me."

"Okay!" Wormie said.

"Antonio Ant, I'm collecting things. Could you help me?" Hermie asked.

"Yes, I will help you, Hermie," Antonio said and tossed **one enormous pine cone** into Hermie's basket.

"Thank you." Hermie smiled. "One enormous pine cone!"

1
one

Hermie looked up and saw Flo the Fly. "Flo, I'm collecting things. Could you help me?"

"Sure!" Flo said.

One!

Two!

Juicy blueberries

landed in Hermie's basket.

"Thank you." Hermie smiled. "Two juicy blueberries!"

2
two

"Annie Ant, I'm collecting things. Could you help me?" Hermie asked.

"Yes, and you can help me," Annie answered. "Take these **three stinky onions**!"

"Thank you." Hermie smiled. "Three stinky onions!"

3
three

"Schneider Snail!" Hermie called. "I'm collecting things. Could you help me?"

"Yes!" Schneider said. "I will give you **four tasty seeds**."

"Thank you." Hermie smiled. "Four tasty seeds!"

4
four

"Wormie, look. Tiny green peas!" Hermie said.

"Don't you have enough in your collection?" Wormie asked.

"No," Hermie answered. "Could you help me?"

"Yes," Wormie said.

One by one, Wormie loaded **five tiny green peas** into Hermie's basket.

"Thank you." Hermie smiled. "Five tiny green peas!"

5
five

"Hermie, what are you doing?" Caitlin Caterpillar asked.

"I'm collecting things. Could you help me?"

"Yes!" said Caitlin. And **six red rose petals** floated gently down into Hermie's basket.

"Mmm, they smell wonderful!" Hermie smiled. "Six red rose petals!"

6
six

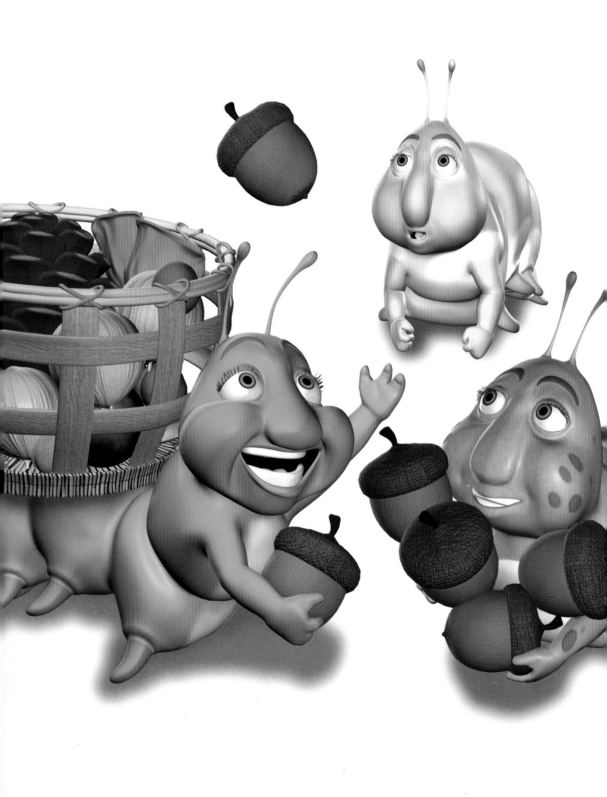

"Hi, Milt! I'm collecting things. Could you help me?" Hermie asked.

"What do you need?"

"Seven special things God made," Hermie said.

"How about some crunchy acorns?" Milt asked.

"Yes, please!"

Milt gave Hermie seven crunchy acorns.

"Thank you." Hermie smiled. "Seven crunchy acorns!"

7

seven

"Hi, Wormie! Hi, Hermie!" Lucy Ladybug waved. "What are you doing?"

"I'm collecting things. Could you help me?" Hermie asked.

"Yes," Lucy said. And with Lucy's help, **eight tender leaves** dropped into Hermie's basket.

"Thank you." Hermie smiled. "Eight tender leaves!"

8
eight

The Ladybug twins, Hailey and Bailey, stared at Hermie and his wobbly load.

"I'm collecting things. Could you help me?" Hermie asked.

"Yes!" Hailey and Bailey said.

But Wormie was worried. Hermie's basket was too full.

Hailey and Bailey added **nine purple grapes** to Hermie's basket.

"Thank you." Hermie smiled. "Nine purple grapes!"

9
nine

Uh-oh! The grapes were too heavy. Hermie and his collection came tumbling down.

Hermie's friends came rushing to see if he was okay. Hermie was not hurt. He got up and looked around.

God had given him the best collection of all—**ten helpful friends**.

"Thank You, God!" Hermie smiled. "Ten helpful friends!"

10
ten

And now Hermie shared with his **10** helpful friends a scrumptious picnic of:

9 purple grapes,

8 tender leaves,

7 crunchy acorns,

6 red rose petals,

5 tiny green peas,

4 tasty seeds,

3 stinky onions,

2 juicy blueberries, and

1 enormous pine cone.

Count with Hermie!

What did Hermie's 10 helpful friends each give him?

Point to each item, say the number and the friend's name.

You can play Hermie's number game anywhere, by counting things that look alike in your home, church, and nature.